Read to Me Mommy

Read to Me Mommy

Selected by

Alistair Hedley

Illustrated by
Kate Aldous, Sue Clarke, Claire Henley, Anna Cynthia Leplar,
Jacqueline Mair, Sheila Moxley, Alan Peacock, Karen Perrins,
Scott Rhodes, Jane Tattersfield, and Sara Walker.

This is a Parragon Publishing Book
This edition published in 2003

Parragon Publishing
Queen Street House
4 Queen Street
Bath BA1 1HE, UK

Created by The Albion Press Ltd

Copyright © Parragon 2000
Selection copyright G Alistair Hedley 2000
Illustrations copyright © Kate Aldous,
Sue Clarke, Claire Henley, Anna Cynthia Leplar,
Jacqueline Mair, Sheila Moxley, Alan Peacock,
Karen Perrins, Scott Rhodes,
Jane Tattersfield, Sara Walker 2000

ISBN 0-75259-486-9

Printed in China

CONTENTS

I SAW THREE SHIPS

I saw three ships come sailing by,
  Come sailing by, come sailing by;
I saw three ships come sailing by,
  On New Year's Day in the morning.

And what do you think was in them then,
  Was in them then, was in them then?
And what do you think was in them then,
  On New Year's Day in the morning?

Three pretty girls were in them then,
  Were in them then, were in them then;
Three pretty girls were in them then,
  On New Year's Day in the morning.

And one could whistle, and one could sing,
  And one could play on the violin—
Such joy there was at my wedding,
  On New Year's Day in the morning.

I SAW A SHIP A-SAILING

I saw a ship a-sailing,
 A-sailing on the sea;
And, oh! it was all laden
 With pretty things for thee!

There were comfits in the cabin,
 And apples in the hold
The sails were made of silk,
 And the masts were made of gold.

The four-and-twenty sailors
 That stood between the decks,
Were four-and-twenty white mice
 With chains about their necks.

The captain was a duck,
 With a packet on his back;
And when the ship began to move,
 The captain said, "Quack! quack!"

THAW

Over the land freckled with show half-thawed
The speculating rooks at their nests cawed
And saw from elm-tops, delicate as flower of grass,
What we below could not see, winter pass.

EDWARD THOMAS

WEATHERS

This is the weather the cuckoo likes,
　　And so do I;
When showers betumble the chestnut spikes,
　　And nestlings fly;
And the little brown nightingale bills his best,
And they sit outside at "The Travellers' Rest,"
And maids come forth spring-muslin drest,
And citizens dream of the south and west,
　　And so do I.

This is the weather the shepherd shuns.
　　And so do I;
When beeches drip in browns and duns,
　　And thresh, and ply;
And hill-hid tides throb, throe on throe,
And meadow rivulets overflow,
And drops on gate-bars hang in a row,
And rooks in families homeward go,
　　And so do I.

THOMAS HARDY

BLOW, BLOW, THOU WINTER WIND

Blow, blow, thou Winter wind,
Thou art not so unkind
    As man's ingratitude;
Thy tooth is not so keen,
Because thou art not seen,
    Although thy breath be rude.
Heigh ho! sing heigh ho! unto the green holly;
Most friendship is feigning, most loving mere folly:
    Then heigh ho, the holly!
    This life is most jolly.

Freeze, freeze, thou bitter sky,
Thou dost not bite so nigh
    As benefits forgot;
Though thou the waters warp,
Thy sting is not so sharp
    As friend remembered not.
Heigh ho! sing heigh ho! unto the green holly;
Most friendship is feigning, most loving mere folly:
    Then heigh ho, the holly!
    This life is most jolly.

WILLIAM SHAKESPEARE

14

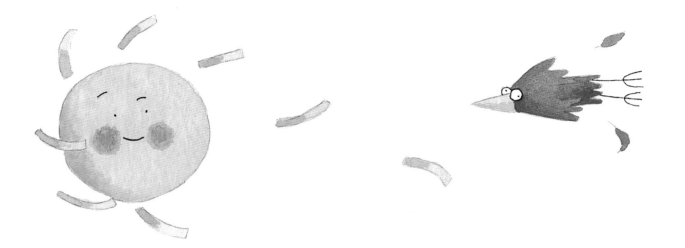

LITTLE WIND

Little wind blow on the hilltop;
Little wind, blow down the plain;
Little wind, blow up the sunshine,
Little wind, blow off the rain.

KATE GREENAWAY

GO TO BED, TOM

Go to bed, Tom,
Go to bed, Tom,
Tired or not, Tom,
Go to bed, Tom.

HIGGLEDY PIGGLEDY

Higgledy piggledy,
Here we lie,
Picked and plucked,
And put in a pie!

WEE WILLIE WINKIE

Wee Willie Winkie runs through the town,
Upstairs and downstairs in his nightgown,
Peeping through the keyhole, crying through the lock,
"Are the children in their beds, it's past eight o'clock?"

THREE WISE MEN OF GOTHAM

Three wise men of Gotham
Went to sea in a bowl:
And if the bowl had been stronger,
My song would have been longer.

JACKANORY

I'll tell you a story
 Of Jackanory,
And now my story's begun;
 I'll tell you another
 Of Jack his brother,
And now my story's done.

FOR EVERY EVIL UNDER THE SUN

For every evil under the sun,
There is a remedy, or there is none.
If there be one, try and find it;
If there be none, never mind it.

SALLY GO ROUND THE MOON

Sally go round the moon,
Sally go round the stars;
Sally go round the moon
On a Sunday afternoon.

STAR LIGHT, STAR BRIGHT

Star light, star bright,
First star I see tonight,
I wish I may, I wish I might,
Have the wish I wish tonight.

THE SAINT
AND
GOD'S CREATURES

Long ago, at the time when the first Christians were building their churches in Wales, there lived a young lad called Baglan. He worked for an old holy man, who was struck by the boy's kindness, and his eagerness to serve God.

One day it was cold and the holy man wanted a fire in his room. So he asked Baglan to move some hot coals to make a fire and to his surprise, the boy carried in some red-hot coals in the fabric of his cloak. When the boy had set the coals in the fire, not a bit of his cloak was burned or even singed.

The old holy man knew a miracle when he saw one. "You are meant to do great works for God," said the holy man. "The time is passed when you should stay here serving me." And the old man produced a crook with a shining brass handle and offered it to the lad. "Take this crook, and set off on a journey. The crook will lead your steps to a place where you must build a church. Look out for a tree which bears three different kinds of fruit. Then you will know that you have come to the right spot."

So the young man took the crook and walked southwards a long way. In time Baglan came to a tree. Around the roots of the tree a family of pigs were grubbing for food. In the tree's trunk had nested a colony of bees. And in the branches of the tree was a nest where a pair of crows were feeding their young.

Baglan sensed that this must be the right place. But the tree grew on sloping land, which did not seem good for building. So the young man looked around until he found a nearby area which was flat, and there he began to build his church.

He worked hard on the first day, digging the foundations, and building the first walls, and he slept well after his labors. But in the morning he was dismayed to see that the walls had all fallen down and water was seeping into the foundation

trenches. So the next day, he worked still harder, and raised the walls stronger and higher than before. But when Baglan awoke the next morning, again the walls had been flattened. He tried once more, putting still greater effort into making his building strong. But again the walls were laid low, and Baglan began to despair of ever finishing his church.

Baglan kneeled down to pray, and then he sat down to think. Perhaps he was not building in exactly the right place. So he moved his site nearer the tree, for the holy man had told him to build where he found the tree with three fruits. Straight

away things began to go better. The pigs, rooting with their snouts, helped him dig out the new foundations. The bees gave him honey. Even the crows offered him crusts of bread that they had scavenged. And this time, Baglan's work was lasting.

So he built and built until his walls surrounded the old tree, leaving windows for the pigs and bees, and a hole in the roof for the birds to fly in and out. As a result, his church looked

rather unusual, but he knew that it was right.

The young man kneeled down and prayed to God in thanks. And when he finished his prayer, he saw that all the animals—the pigs, and the bees, and the crows—had also fallen still and silent, as if they too, were thanking God that the work was completed.

After that, Baglan was always kind to the animals, and taught others to show kindness to them also. His crook may have been a holy relic that guided him to the tree, but even it could be used to scratch the back of the great boar.

WHEN FAMED KING ARTHUR RULED THIS LAND

When famed King Arthur ruled this land
  He was a goodly king:
He took three pecks of barley meal
  To make a bag pudding.

A rare pudding the king did make,
  And stuffed it well with plums;
And in it put such lumps of fat,
  As big as my two thumbs.

The king and queen did eat thereof,
  And noblemen beside,
And what they could not eat that night
  The queen next morning fried.

WHAT IS THE RHYME FOR PORRINGER?

What is the rhyme for *porringer*?
The King he had a daughter fair,
And gave the Prince of Orange her.

GRAY GOOSE AND GANDER

Gray goose and gander,
  Waft your wings together,
And carry the good king's daughter
  Over the one strand river.

OLIVER TWIST

Oliver Twist
You can't do this,
So what's the use
Of trying?
Touch your toe,
Touch your knee,
Clap your hands,
Away we go.

A SAILOR WENT TO SEA

A sailor went to sea, sea, sea,

To see what he could see, see, see,

But all that he could see, see, see,

Was the bottom of the deep blue sea, sea, sea.

LITTLE SALLY WATERS

Little Sally Waters,
Sitting in the sun,
Crying and weeping,
For a young man.
Rise, Sally, rise,
Dry your weeping eyes,
Fly to the east,
Fly to the west,
Fly to the one you love the best.

MR. NOBODY

Mr. Nobody is a nice young man,

He comes to the door with his hat in his hand.

Down she comes, all dressed in silk,

A rose in her bosom, as white as milk.

She takes off her gloves, she shows me her ring,

Tomorrow, tomorrow, the wedding begins.

HAVE YOU SEEN THE MUFFIN MAN

Have you seen the muffin man, the muffin man, the
  muffin man,
Have you seen the muffin man that lives in Drury
  Lane O?
Yes, I've seen the muffin man, the muffin man, the
  muffin man;
Yes, I've seen the muffin man who lives in Drury
  Lane O.

OLD ROGER IS DEAD

Old Roger is dead and
  gone to his grave,
H'm ha! gone to his grave.

They planted an apple tree
  over his head,
H'm ha! over his head.

The apples were ripe
  and ready to fall,
H'm ha! ready to fall.

There came an old woman
  and picked them all up,
H'm ha! picked them all up.

Old Roger jumped up and
  gave her a knock,
H'm ha! gave her a knock.

Which made the old woman
  go hippity hop,
H'm ha! hippity hop!

SNEEZE ON MONDAY

Sneeze on Monday, sneeze for danger;
Sneeze on Tuesday, kiss a stranger;
Sneeze on Wednesday, get a letter;
Sneeze on Thursday, something better;
Sneeze on Friday, sneeze for sorrow;
Sneeze on Saturday, see your sweetheart
  tomorrow.

SEE A PIN AND PICK IT UP

See a pin and pick it up,
All the day you'll have good luck;
See a pin and let it lay,
Bad luck you'll have all the day!

RAIN, RAIN, GO AWAY

Rain, rain, go away,
Come again another day.

THE LION AND THE UNICORN

The lion and the unicorn
　　Were fighting for the crown:
The lion beat the unicorn
　　All round the town.
Some gave them white bread,
　　Some gave them brown:
Some gave them plum-cake
　　And drummed them out of town.

POP GOES THE WEASEL

Up and down the City Road
   In and out the Eagle,
That's the way the money goes,
   Pop goes the weasel!

Half a pound of tuppenny rice,
   Half a pound of treacle,
Mix it up and make it nice,
   Pop goes the weasel!

Every night when I go out
   The monkey's on the table;
Take a stick and knock it off,
   Pop goes the weasel!

THERE WAS AN OLD MAN WITH A BEARD

There was an old Man with a beard,
Who said, "It is just as I feared!—
Two Owls and a Hen, four Larks and a Wren
Have all built their nests in my beard!"

EDWARD LEAR

THERE WAS AN OLD MAN FROM PERU

There was an old man from Peru
Who dreamed he was eating his shoe.
He woke in a fright
In the middle of the night
And found it was perfectly true.

ANONYMOUS
ENGLISH

38

OZYMANDIAS

I met a traveller from an antique land
Who said: Two vast and trunkless legs of stone
Stand in the desert....Near them, on the sand,
Half sunk, a shattered visage lies, whose frown,
And wrinkled lip, and sneer of cold command,
Tell that its sculptor well those passions read
Which yet survive, stamped on these lifeless things,
The hand that mocked them, and the heart that fed:
And on the pedestal these words appear:
"My name is Ozymandias, king of kings:
Look on my works, ye Mighty, and despair!"
Nothing beside remains. Round the decay
Of that colossal wreck, boundless and bare
The lone and level sands stretch far away.

PERCY BYSSHE SHELLEY

WHEN THAT I WAS AND A LITTLE TINY BOY

When that I was and a little tiny boy,
   With hey, ho, the wind and the rain;
A foolish thing was but a toy,
   For the rain it raineth every day.

But when I came to man's estate,
   With hey, ho, the wind and the rain;
'Gainst knaves and thieves men shut their gate,
   For the rain it raineth every day.

A great while ago the world begun,
   With hey, ho, the wind and the rain;
But that's all one, our play is done,
   And we'll strive to please you every day.

WILLIAM SHAKESPEARE

I EAT MY PEAS WITH HONEY

I eat my peas with honey,
I've done it all my life,
It makes the peas taste funny,
But it keeps them on my knife.

ANONYMOUS
AMERICAN

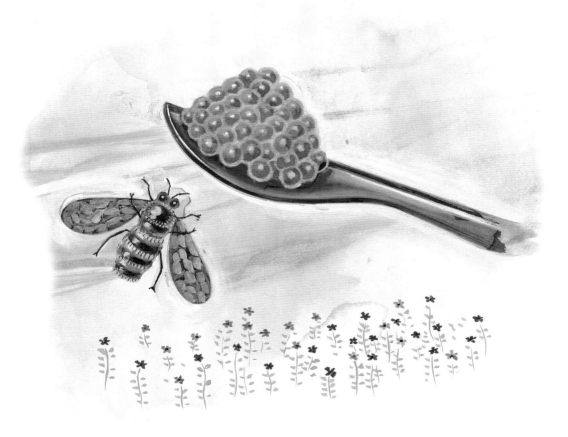

41

BREAD AND MILK FOR BREAKFAST

Bread and milk for breakfast,
    And woollen frocks to wear,
And a crumb for robin redbreast
    On the cold days of the year.

CHRISTINA ROSSETTI

WINDY NIGHTS

Whenever the moon and stars are set,
  Whenever the wind is high,
All night long in the dark and wet,
  A man goes riding by
Late in the night when the fires are out,
Why does he gallop and gallop about?

Whenever the trees are crying aloud,
  And ships are tossed at sea,
By, on the highway, low and loud,
  By at the gallop goes he.
But at the gallop he goes, and then
By he comes back at the gallop again.

ROBERT LOUIS STEVENSON

MUNACHAR AND MANACHAR

There were once two little fellows called Munachar and Manachar. They liked to pick raspberries, but Manachar always ate them all. Munachar got so fed up with this that he said he would look for a rod to make a gibbet to hang Manachar.

Soon, Munachar came to a rod. "What do you want?" said the rod. "A rod, to make a gibbet," replied Munachar.

"You won't get me," said the rod, "unless you can get an ax to cut me." So Munachar went to find an ax. "What do you want?" said the ax. "I am looking for an ax, to cut a rod, to make a gibbet," replied Munachar.

"You won't get me," said the ax, "unless you can get a stone to sharpen me." So Munachar went to find a stone. "What do you want?" said the stone. "I am looking for a stone, to sharpen an ax, to cut a rod, to make a gibbet," replied Munachar.

"You won't get me," said the stone, "unless you can get water to wet me." So Munachar went to find water. "What do you want?" said the water. "I am looking for water to wet a stone, to sharpen an ax, to cut a rod, to make a gibbet," replied Munachar.

"You won't get me," said the water, "unless you can get a deer who will swim me." So Munachar went to look for a deer. "What do you want?" said the deer. "I am looking for a deer, to swim some water, to wet a stone, to sharpen an ax, to cut a rod, to make a gibbet," replied Munachar.

"You won't get me," said the deer, "unless you can get a hound who will hunt me." So Munachar went to look for a hound. "What do you want?" said the hound. "I am looking for a hound, to hunt a deer, to swim some water, to wet a stone, to sharpen an ax, to cut a rod, to make a gibbet," replied Munachar.

"You won't get me," said the hound, "unless you can get some butter to put in my claw." So Munachar went to look for some butter. "What do you want?" said the butter. "I am looking for some butter to put in the claw of a hound, to hunt a deer, to swim some water, to wet a stone, to sharpen an ax, to cut a rod, to make a gibbet," replied Munachar.

"You won't get me," said the butter, "unless you can get a cat who can scrape me." So Munachar went to look for a cat.

"What do you want?" said the cat. "I am looking for a cat to scrape some butter, to put in the claw of a hound, to hunt a deer, to swim some water, to wet a stone, to sharpen an ax, to cut a rod, to make a gibbet, " replied Munachar.

"You won't get me," said the cat, "unless you can get some milk to feed me." So Munachar went to get some milk. "What do you want?" said the milk. "I am looking for some milk, to feed a cat, to scrape some butter, to put in the claw of a hound, to hunt a deer, to swim some water, to wet a stone, to sharpen an ax, to cut a rod, to make a gibbet," replied Munachar.

"You won't get me," said the milk, "unless you can bring me some straw from those threshers over there." So Munachar went to ask the threshers. "What do you want?" said the threshers. "I am looking for some straw, to give to the milk, to feed a cat, to scrape some butter, to put in the claw of a hound, to hunt a deer, to swim some water, to wet a stone, to sharpen an ax, to cut a rod, to make a gibbet," replied Munachar.

"You won't get any straw," said the threshers, "unless you

bring some flour to bake a cake from the miller next door." So Munachar went to ask the miller. "What do you want?" said the miller. "I am looking for some flour to bake a cake, to give to the threshers, to get some straw, to give to the milk, to feed a cat, to scrape some butter, to put in the claw of a hound, to hunt a deer, to swim some water, to wet a stone, to sharpen an ax, to cut a rod, to make a gibbet," replied Munachar.

"You'll get no flour ," said the miller, "unless you fill this sieve with water." Some crows flew over crying "Daub! Daub!" So Munachar daubed some clay on the sieve, so it would hold water.

And he took the water to the miller, who gave him the flour; he gave the flour to the threshers, who gave him some straw; he took the straw to the cow, who gave him some milk; he took the milk to the cat, who scraped some butter; he gave the butter to the hound, who hunted the deer; the deer swam the water; the water wet the stone; the stone sharpened the ax; the ax cut the rod; the rod made a gibbet – and when Munachar was ready to hang Manachar, he found that Manachar had BURST!

I LOVE LITTLE PUSSY

I love little pussy, her coat is so warm;
And if I don't hurt her she'll do me no harm.
So I'll not pull her tail nor drive her away,
But pussy and I very gently will play.

PUSSYCAT MOLE

Pussycat Mole,
Jumped over a coal,
And in her best petticoat burnt a great hole.
Poor pussy's weeping, she'll have no more milk,
Until her best petticoat's mended with silk.

PUSSYCAT, PUSSYCAT

Pussycat, pussycat, where have you been?

I've been to London to see the Queen.

Pussycat, pussycat, what did you there?

I frightened a little mouse under her chair.

JACK, JACK, THE BREAD'S A-BURNING

Jack, Jack, the bread's a-burning,
All to a cinder;
If you don't come and fetch it out
We'll throw it through the window.

JACK AND GUY

Jack and Guy
  Went out in the rye,
And they found a little boy with one black eye.
Come, says Jack, let's knock him on the head.
No, says Guy, let's buy him some bread;
You buy one loaf and I'll buy two,
And we'll bring him up as other folk do.

JACK AND JILL

Jack and Jill went up the hill
  To fetch a pail of water;
Jack fell down and broke his crown,
  And Jill came tumbling after.

Up Jack got, and home did trot,
  As fast as he could caper,
Went to bed to mend his head
  With vinegar and brown paper.

LITTLE JACK JINGLE

Little Jack Jingle,
He used to live single:
But when he got tired of this kind of life,
He left off being single, and lived with his wife.

HARRY PARRY

O rare Harry Parry,
When will you marry?
When apples and pears are ripe.
I'll come to your wedding,
Without any bidding,
And dance and sing all the night.

YOUNG ROGER CAME TAPPING

Young Roger came tapping at Dolly's window,
  Thumpaty, thumpaty, thump!
He asked for admittance, she answered him "No!"
  Frumpaty, frumpaty, frump!

"No, no, Roger, no! as you came you may go!"
  Stumpaty, stumpaty, stump!

SOLOMON GRUNDY

Solomon Grundy,
Born on Monday,
Christened on Tuesday,
Married on Wednesday,
Sick on Thursday,
Worse on Friday,
Died on Saturday,
Buried on Sunday,
That was the end
Of Solomon Grundy.

OLD KING COLE

Old King Cole
Was a merry old soul,
And a merry old soul was he;
He called for his pipe,
And he called for his bowl,
And he called for his fiddlers three.
Every fiddler had a fine fiddle,
And a very fine fiddle had he;
Twee tweedle dee, tweedle dee, went the fiddlers,
    Very merry men are we;
    Oh there's none so rare
    As can compare
With King Cole and his fiddlers three.

BOBBIE SHAFTOE'S GONE TO SEA

Bobbie Shaftoe's gone to sea,
Silver buckles at his knee;
When he comes back he'll marry me,
Bonny Bobbie Shaftoe!

PUSSY HAS A WHISKERED FACE

Pussy has a whiskered face,
Kitty has such pretty ways;
Doggie scampers when I call,
And has a heart to love us all.

JOHNNY SHALL HAVE A NEW BONNET

Johnny shall have a new bonnet,
And Johnny shall go to the fair,
And Johnny shall have a blue ribbon
To tie up his bonny brown hair.

THE MISSING KETTLE

There was a woman who lived on the island of Sanntraigh, and she had only a kettle to hang over the fire to boil her water and cook her food. Every day one of the fairy folk would come to take the kettle. She would slip into the house quietly without saying a word, and grab hold of the kettle handle.

Each time this happened, the kettle handle made a clanking noise and the woman looked up and recited this rhyme:

A smith is able to make

Cold iron hot with coal.

The due of a kettle is bones,

And to bring it back again whole.

Then the fairy would fly away with the kettle and the woman would not see it again until later in the day, when the fairy brought it back, filled with flesh and bones.

There came at last a day when the woman had to leave home and go on the ferry across to the mainland. She turned to her husband, who was making a rope of heather to keep the thatch on the roof. "Will you say the rhyme that I say when the fairy comes for the kettle?" Her husband said that he would recite the rhyme just as she did, and went back to his work.

After the woman had left to catch the boat, the fairy arrived as usual, and the husband saw her come to the door. When he saw her he started to feel afraid, for unlike his wife he had had no contact with the little people. "If I lock the cottage door," he reasoned to himself, "she will go away and leave the kettle, and it will be just as if she had never come." So the husband locked the door and did not open it when the fairy tried to come in.

But instead of going away, the fairy flew up to the hole in the roof where the smoke from the fire escaped, and before the husband knew what was happening, the creature had made the kettle jump right up and out of the

hole. The fairy made away with the kettle before he knew what to do.

When his wife returned that evening, there was no kettle to be seen.

"What have you done with my kettle?" asked the woman.

"I've done nothing with it," said the husband. "But I took fright when the fairy came, closed the door to her, she took the kettle through the roof, and now it is gone."

"You pathetic wretch! Can't you even mind the kettle when I go out for the day?"

The husband tried to tell his wife that the fairy might return the kettle the next day, but the woman would hear nothing of it. Off she went straight away to the knoll where the fairies lived, to see if she could get back the kettle herself.

It was quite dark when she reached the fairies' knoll. The hillside opened to her and when she went in she saw only an old fairy sitting in the corner. The woman supposed that the others were out at their nightly mischief. Soon she found her kettle, and noticed that it still contained the remains of the food the little people had cooked in it.

She picked up the kettle and ran back down the lane, when she heard the sound of dogs chasing her. The old fairy must have let them loose. Thinking quickly, she took out some of the food from the kettle, threw it to the dogs, and hurried on.

This slowed down the dogs, and when they began to catch her up again, she threw down more food. Finally, when she got near her own gate, she poured out the rest of the food, hoping that the dogs would not come into her own house. Then she ran inside and closed the door.

Every day after that the woman watched for the fairy coming to take her kettle. But the little creature never came again.

OLD JOE BROWN

Old Joe Brown, he had a wife,
She was all of eight feet tall.
She slept with her head in the kitchen,
And her feet stuck out in the hall.

THE MONTHS

Thirty days hath September,
April, June, and November;
All the rest have thirty-one,
Excepting February alone,
And that has twenty-eight days clear
And twenty-nine in each leap year.

DANDY

I had a dog and his name was Dandy,
His tail was long and his legs were bandy,
His eyes were brown and his coat was sandy,
The best in the world was my dog Dandy!

FUZZY WUZZY

Fuzzy Wuzzy was a bear,
  A bear was Fuzzy Wuzzy.
When Fuzzy Wuzzy lost his hair
  He wasn't fuzzy, was he?

THE SWING

How do you like to go up in a swing,
  Up in the air so blue?
Oh, I do think it the pleasantest thing
  Ever a child can do!

Up in the air and over the wall,
  Till I can see so wide,
Rivers and trees and cattle and all
  Over the countryside—

Till I look down on the garden green,
  Down on the roof so brown—
Up in the air I go flying again,
  Up in the air and down!

ROBERT LOUIS STEVENSON

THE CITY CHILD

Dainty little maiden, whither would you wander?
  Whither from this pretty home, the home where
    mother dwells?
"Far and far away," said the dainty little maiden,
"All among the gardens, auriculas, anemones,
  Roses and lilies and Canterbury-bells."

Dainty little maiden, whither would you wander?
  Whither from this pretty house, this city house
    of ours?
"Far and far away," said the dainty little maiden,
"All among the meadows, the clover and the clematis,
  Daisies and kingcups and honeysuckle-flowers."

ALFRED, LORD TENNYSON

65

TOMMY SNOOKS AND BESSY BROOKS

As Tommy Snooks and Bessy Brooks
Were walking out one Sunday,
Says Tommy Snooks to Bessy Brooks,
"Tomorrow will be Monday."

LITTLE JUMPING JOAN

Here am I, little jumping Joan.
When nobody's with me,
I'm always alone.

THERE WAS A LITTLE GIRL

There was a little girl, and she had a little curl
    Right in the middle of her forehead;
When she was good she was very, very good,
    But when she was bad she was horrid.

ANNA BANANA

Anna Banana
Played the piano;
The piano broke
And Anna choked.

LUCY LOCKET

Lucy Locket lost her pocket,
Kitty Fisher found it,
But not a penny was there in it
Just the binding round it

LITTLE MISS MUFFET

Little Miss Muffet
Sat on a tuffet,
Eating her curds and whey;
There came a great spider,
Who sat down beside her,
And frightened Miss Muffet away.

THE
BLACK LAD MacCRIMMON

There was once a young man called the Black Lad MacCrimmon. He was the youngest of three brothers and he was the most downtrodden of the three. His elder brothers were always favored by their father, and were always given more food, and allowed more enjoyment, than the Black Lad. The Black Lad, on the other hand, was always given the hardest jobs to do when the four were working together.

The father and the elder brothers were all great pipers, and they had a fine set of pipes that they liked to play. The Black Lad would have liked to have played the pipes too, but he was never allowed. Always the brothers took up too much time with their playing to give the young lad a chance.

In those days, people said that the greatest musicians of all were the fairy folk. The Black Lad hoped that one day he would meet one of the little people and they would teach him to master the pipes.

The day came that the lad's father and his two brothers were getting ready to go to the fair. The Black Lad wanted to go too, but they would not take him. So the lad stayed at home, and when they were gone, he decided to take up the chanter from the set of pipes and see if he could play a tune.

After a while of practising, the lad began to pick out a tune on the chanter. He was starting to enjoy himself, and was so absorbed in what he was doing that he did not notice that someone was watching him and listening.

Suddenly a voice spoke in his ear: "You are doing well with your music, lad." It was none other than the Banshee from the castle.

"Which would you prefer," continued the Banshee. "Skill without success or success without skill?"

The lad replied that what he wanted most of all was skill, it did not matter about success. The Banshee smiled, as if she approved of the answer, and pulled a long hair from her head. This she wound around the reed of the chanter. Then she turned to the Black Lad MacCrimmon. "Now put your fingers on the holes of the chanter, and I will place my fingers over yours. I will guide you. When I lift one of my fingers, you lift yours that is beneath it. Think of a tune that you would like to play, and I will help you play. And my skill will rub off on you."

So the lad began to play, guided by the Banshee as she had told him. Soon he was playing with great skill, and he could master any tune that he thought of.

"Indeed you are the King of the Pipers," said the Banshee. "There has been none better before you, and none better shall come after." And with this blessing, the Banshee went on her way back to the castle.

The Black Lad carried on playing when she had left, and he could play all the tunes that he tried. When his father and

brothers returned, they could
hear him playing as they came
along the road, but by the time
they entered the house, the lad
had put away the pipes, and
was acting as if nothing at all
had happened.

None of them mentioned that
they had heard music when
they came in, but the lad's
father took down the pipes, and
played as usual. Then he hand-
ed them to his first son, who played and passed them to the
second son. But instead of putting the pipes away after his
second son had played, old MacCrimmon handed the pipes
to his youngest son. "Now take the pipes, for no longer shall
you spend all day doing the hardest of the work and eating
the meanest of the food."

When the lad played, they heard that he was far better than
any of them. "There is no longer any point in our playing,"
said the father to the two eldest sons. "The lad is truly King
of the Pipers." And the lad's brothers knew that what their
father said was true.

TOM, TOM, THE PIPER'S SON

Tom, Tom, the piper's son,
Stole a pig, and away he run.
The pig was eat, and Tom was beat,
And Tom went roaring down the street.

TOM, HE WAS A PIPER'S SON

Tom, he was a piper's son,
He learnt to play when he was young,
And all the tune that he could play,
Was, "Over the hills and far away."

Over the hills and a great way off,
The wind shall blow my topknot off.

Tom with his pipe made such a noise
That he pleased both the girls and boys,
And they all stopped to hear him play
"Over the hills and far away."

Over the hills and a great way off,
The wind shall blow my topknot off.

ELSIE MARLEY

Elsie Marley is grown so fine,
She won't get up to serve the swine,
But lies in bed till eight or nine,
And surely she does take her time.

MARY, MARY

Mary, Mary, quite contrary,
How does your garden grow?
With silver bells, and cockle shells,
And pretty maids all in a row.

POLLY, PUT THE KETTLE ON

Polly, put the kettle on,
Polly, put the kettle on,
Polly, put the kettle on,
　And we'll all have tea.

Sukey, take it off again,
Sukey, take it off again,
Sukey, take it off again,
　They're all gone

A PRETTY LITTLE GIRL

A pretty little girl in a round-eared cap
I met in the streets the other day;
   She gave me such a thump,
   That my heart it went bump;
I thought I should have fainted away!
I thought I should have fainted away!

THE FARMER
AND
THE GOAT GIRL

There was once a farmer called Cadwalader. Unlike all his neighbors, who were sheep farmers, Cadwalader had a large flock of goats. Of all his goats he had a special favorite that he called Jenny, and Jenny was the whitest and most beautiful of all his flock.

For many years Jenny was Cadwalader's best milk producer, and she was always obedient, unlike some of the stubborn  creatures in his flock. Then, one day, Jenny bolted from the field and ran away. Up the nearest mountain she went, and seemed not to be stopping, so Cadwalader gave chase.

They climbed higher and higher, Jenny always slightly ahead. When it seemed as if the farmer would catch her, she jumped on to a nearby crag, leaving Cadwalader stranded.

Not only did the farmer feel stupid, stuck on the mountain like this, he also collected bruises and sprains as he clambered among the rocks. Finally, he had had enough, and he picked up a stone and hurled it at the goat in frustration as she was jumping another chasm.

The stone hit Jenny in the side, and, bleating loudly, she fell far down into the gap between the rocks. Straight away Cadwalader was full of remorse. It was only in a moment of frustration that he had wanted to hurt the animal, and now his only wish was to see that she was still alive. He clambered down to the rocky gap where she lay, and saw that, although she was still breathing, she was badly injured. He did his best to make her comfortable, and tears of sadness formed in his eyes as he saw how she was hurt.

It was now dark, but the moon appeared between the rocks and shed its light on the scene. As the moon rose, the goat turned into a beautiful young woman who was lying there before Cadwalader. He looked in bafflement at her brown eyes and soft hair, and

81

found that not only was she beautiful, she was also well and looked pleased to see him. "So, my dear Cadwalader," she said. "At long last I can speak to you."

Cadwalader did not know what to make of all this. When the young woman spoke, there seemed to be a bleat in her voice; when she held his hand, it felt like a hoof. Was she goat or girl, or some strange mixture of the two?

As she led him towards an outcrop of rock, Cadwalader felt he was heading into danger. As they rounded a corner, they found themselves surrounded by a flock of goats—not the tame creatures Cadwalader was used to, but large wild goats,

many of which had long horns and beards. Jenny led him to the largest goat of all, and bowed, as if he were a king.

"Is this the man you want?" the goat asked Jenny.

"Yes, he is the one."

"Not a very fine specimen," said the goat-king. "I had hoped for something better"

"He will be better afterwards," replied Jenny.

Cadwalader wondered what was going to happen, and looked around him in fear. Then the goat-king turned to Cadwalader.

"Will you, Cadwalader, take this she-goat to be your wife?"

"No, my lord. I want nothing to do with goats ever again." And with that, Cadwalader turned and ran for his life. He was fast, but not fast enough for the great goat-king. Coming up behind Cadwalader, the huge billy goat gave the farmer such a tremendous butt that Cadwalader fell headlong down the crag, rolling and falling, falling and rolling, until he came to a stop, unconscious, right at the bottom of the mountain.

There Cadwalader lay for the rest of the night, until he woke, aching from head to toe, at dawn. He limped home to his farm, where his goats bleated in welcome. But Cadwalader wanted to be a goat farmer no more. He drove his goats to market, and bought a flock of sheep, just like his neighbors.

HURT NO LIVING THING

Hurt no living thing,
 Ladybug nor butterfly,
Nor moth with dusty wing,
Nor cricket chirping cheerily,
Nor grasshopper, so light of leap,
 Nor dancing gnat,
 Nor beetle fat,
Nor harmless worms that creep.

CHRISTINA ROSSETTI

THE COW

The friendly cow all red and white,
  I love with all my heart:
She gives me cream with all her might,
  To eat with appletart.

She wanders lowing here and there,
  And yet she cannot stray,
All in the pleasant open air,
  The pleasant light of day;

And blown by all the winds that pass
  And wet with all the showers,
She walks among the meadow grass
  And eats the meadow flowers.

ROBERT LOUIS STEVENSON

TO A BUTTERFLY

I've watched you now a full half-hour,
Self-poised upon that yellow flower;
And, little Butterfly! indeed
I know not if you sleep or feed.
How motionless!—not frozen seas
More motionless! And then
What joy awaits you, when the breeze
Hath found you out among the trees,
And calls you forth again!

This plot of orchard-ground is ours;
My trees they are, my Sister's flowers.
Here rest your wings when they are weary;
Here lodge as in a sanctuary!
Come often to us, fear no wrong;
Sit near us on the bough!
We'll talk of sunshine and of song,
And summer days, when we were young;
Sweet childish days, that were as long
As twenty days are now.

WILLIAM WORDSWORTH

CATERPILLAR

Brown and furry

Caterpillar in a hurry,

Take your walk

To the shady leaf, or stalk,

Or what not,

Which may be the chosen spot.

No toad spy you,

Hovering bird of prey pass by you;

Spin and die,

To live again a butterfly.

CHRISTINA ROSSETTI

WASH, HANDS, WASH

Wash, hands, wash,
  Daddy's gone to plow;
If you want your hands washed,
  Have them washed now.

CLAP HANDS

Clap hands for Daddy coming
Down the wagon way,
With a pocketful of money
And a cartload of hay.

THE GREAT BROWN OWL

The brown owl sits in the ivy bush,
　And she looketh wondrous wise,
With a horny beak beneath her cowl,
　And a pair of large round eyes.

She sat all day on the selfsame spray,
　From sunrise till sunset;
And the dim, grey light it was all too bright
　For the owl to see in yet.

"Jenny Owlet, Jenny Owlet," said a merry little bird,
　"They say you're wondrous wise;
But I don't think you see, though you're looking at *me*
　With your large, round, shining eyes."

But night came soon, and the pale white moon
　Rolled high up in the skies;
And the great brown owl flew away in her cowl,
　With her large, round, shining eyes.

AUNT EFFIE (JANE EUPHEMIA BROWNE)

THE OWL

When cats run home and light is come,
  And dew is cold upon the ground,
And the far-off stream is dumb,
  And the whirring sail goes round,
  And the whirring sail goes round;
   Alone and warming his five wits,
  The white owl in the belfry sits.

When merry milkmaids click the latch,
  And rarely smells the new-mown hay,
And the cock hath sung beneath the thatch
  Twice or thrice his roundelay,
  Twice or thrice his roundelay;
   Alone and warming his five wits,
  The white owl in the belfry sits.

ALFRED, LORD TENNYSON

LITTLE TROTTY WAGTAIL

Little Trotty Wagtail, he went in the rain,
And twittering, tottering sideways, he ne'er got
  straight again;
He stooped to get a worm, and looked up to get a fly,
And then he flew away ere his feathers they were dry.

Little Trotty Wagtail, he waddled in the mud,
And left his little footmarks, trample where he would,
He waddled in the water-pudge, and waggle went his tail,
And chirrupped up his wings to dry upon the garden rail.

Little Trotty Wagtail, you nimble all about,
And in the dimpling water-pudge you waddle in and out;
Your home is nigh at hand and in the warm pigsty;
So, little Master Wagtail, I'll bid you a goodby.

JOHN CLARE

EPIGRAM

Engraved on the Collar of a Dog which I Gave to His
Royal Highness

I am his Highness' Dog at Kew:
Pray tell me, sir, whose dog are you?

ALEXANDER POPE

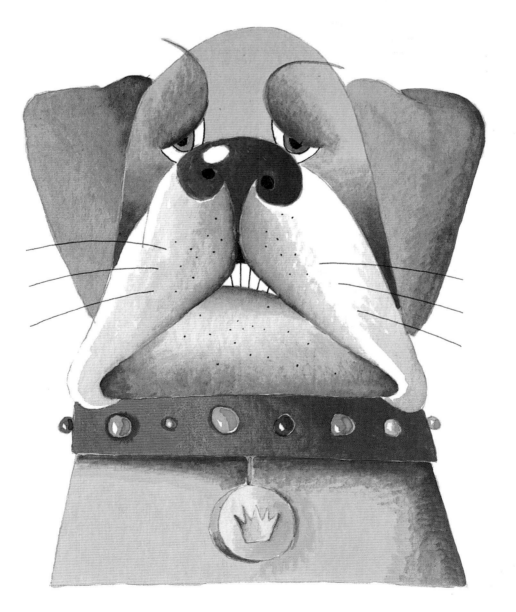

BLOW, WIND, BLOW!

Blow, wind, blow! and go, mill, go!
That the miller may grind his corn;
　That the baker may take it,
　And into rolls make it,
And send us some hot in the morn.

PAT-A-CAKE, PAT-A-CAKE BAKER'S MAN!

Pat-a-cake, pat-a-cake, baker's man!
　Bake me a cake, as fast as you can;
Pat it and prick it, and mark it with T,
　And put it aside for Tommy and me.

HOT-CROSS BUNS

Hot-Cross Buns!
Hot-Cross Buns!
One a penny, two a penny,
Hot-Cross Buns!

Hot-Cross Buns!
Hot-Cross Buns!
If you have no daughters
Give them to your sons.

ONCE I SAW A LITTLE BIRD

Once I saw a little bird
Come hop, hop, hop;
So I cried, "Little bird,
Will you stop, stop, stop?"
And was going to the window,
To say, "How do you do?"
But he shook his little tail,
And far away he flew.

JAY-BIRD

Jay-bird, jay-bird, settin' on a rail,
Pickin' his teeth with the end of his tail;
Mulberry leaves and calico sleeves—
All school teachers are hard to please.

BIRDS OF A FEATHER

Birds of a feather flock together
And so will pigs and swine;
Rats and mice shall have their choice,
And so shall I have mine.

TIGGY-TOUCHWOOD

Tiggy-tiggy-touchwood, my black hen,
She lays eggs for gentlemen,
Sometimes nine and sometimes ten,
Tiggy-tiggy-touchwood, my black hen.

I HAD A LITTLE HEN

I had a little hen, the prettiest ever seen,
She washed me the dishes, and kept the house clean:
She went to the mill to fetch me some flour,
She brought it home in less than an hour;
She baked me my bread, she brewed me my ale,
She sat by the fire and told many a fine tale.

MRS HEN

Chook, chook, chook, chook, chook,
   Good morning, Mrs Hen.
How many chickens have you got?
   Madam, I've got ten.

Four of them are yellow,
   And four of them are brown,
And two of them are speckled red,
   The nicest in the town.

BAA, BAA, BLACK SHEEP

Baa, baa, black sheep, have you any wool?
Yes, sir; yes, sir, three bags full:
One for the master, one for the dame,
And one for the little boy that lives down the lane.

MARY HAD A LITTLE LAMB

Mary had a little lamb,
Its fleece was white as snow,
And everywhere that Mary went
The lamb was sure to go.

It followed her to school one day,
Which was against the rule;
It made the children laugh and play
To see a lamb in school.

CUSHY COW BONNY

Cushy cow bonny, let down thy milk,
And I will give thee a gown of silk;
A gown of silk and a silver tree,
If thou wilt let down thy milk to me.

I HAD A LITTLE COW

I had a little cow;
  Hey-diddle, ho-diddle!
I had a little cow, and it had a little calf;
Hey-diddle, ho-diddle; and there's my song half.

I had a little cow;
  Hey-diddle, ho-diddle!
I had a little cow, and I drove it to the stall;
Hey-diddle, ho-diddle; and there's my song all!

THERE WAS A PIPER, HE'D A COW

There was a piper, he'd a cow,
    And he'd no hay to give her;
He took his pipes and played a tune:
    "Consider, old cow, consider!"

The cow considered very well,
    For she gave the piper a penny,
That he might play the tune again,
    Of "Corn rigs are bonnie."

WAY DOWN YONDER IN THE MAPLE SWAMP

Way down yonder in the maple swamp
The wild geese gather and the ganders honk
The mares kick up and the ponies prance;
The old sow whistles and the little pigs dance.

BETTY PRINGLE

Betty Pringle had a little pig,
Not very little and not very big;
When he was alive he lived in clover;
But now he's dead, and that's all over.
So Billy Pringle he laid down and cried,
And Betty Pringle she laid down and died;
So there was an end of one, two, and three:
    Billy Pringle he,
    Betty Pringle she,a
    And the piggy wiggy.

THE DAYS ARE CLEAR

The days are clear,
  Day after day,
When April's here
  That leads to May,
And June
Must follow soon:
  Stay, June, stay!—
If only we could stop the moon
And June!

CHRISTINA ROSETTI

ITSY BITSY SPIDER

Itsy Bitsy spider
  Climbing up the spout;
Down came the rain
  And washed the spider out:
Out came the sunshine
  And dried up all the rain;
Itsy Bitsy spider
  Climbing up again.

THE
HUMBLE-BEE

Two young men were out walking one summer's day and stopped by a tiny stream next to an old ruined house. They were admiring the place, and noticed how the stream turned into a miniature waterfall crossed by narrow blades of grass. One of the men was tired from the walk and the afternoon heat and sat down by the stream. Soon he was fast asleep, and the other sat quietly, watching the view.

Suddenly, a tiny creature, about the size of a humble-bee, flew out of the sleeper's mouth. It landed by the stream and crossed it by walking over some grass stalks which hung over the water at its narrowest point. The creature then approached the ruin and disappeared into one of the cracks in the wall.

The man who saw all this was shocked and decided to wake his friend to see if he was all right. As he shook his companion awake, he was astonished to see the tiny creature emerge from the ruin, fly across the stream and re-enter the sleeper's mouth, just as the young man was waking.

"What's the matter? Are you ill?" asked the watcher.

"I am well," replied the sleeper. "You have just interrupted the most wonderful dream, and I wish you had not woken me

with your shaking. I dreamed that I walked through a vast grassy plain and came to a wide river. I wanted to cross the river to see what was on the other side, and I found a place near a great waterfall where there was a bridge made of silver. I walked over the bridge and on the far bank was a beautiful palace built of stone. When I looked in, the chambers of the palace contained great mounds of gold and jewels. I was looking at all these fine things, wondering at the wealth of the person who left them there, and deciding which I would bring away with me. Then suddenly you woke me, and I could bring away none of the riches."

BOW, WOW, WOW

Bow, wow, wow,
   Whose dog art thou?
"Little Tom Tinker's dog,
   Bow, wow, wow."

TWO LITTLE DOGS

Two little dogs
   Sat by the fire
Over a fender of coal-dust;
   Said one little dog
   To the other little dog,
If you don't talk, why, I must.

PUSSYCAT SITS BY THE FIRE

Pussycat sits by the fire.
　　How did she come there?
In walks the little dog,
　　Says, "Pussy! are you there?
How do you do, Mistress Pussy?
　　Mistress Pussy, how d'ye do?"
"I thank you kindly, little dog,
　　I fare as well as you!"

ROBIN AND RICHARD

Robin and Richard were two pretty men;
They laid in bed till the clock struck ten;
Then up starts Robin and looks at the sky,
Oh! brother Richard, the sun's very high:

The bull's in the barn threshing the corn,
The rooster's on the dunghill blowing his horn,
The cat's at the fire frying of fish,
The dog's in the pantry breaking his dish.

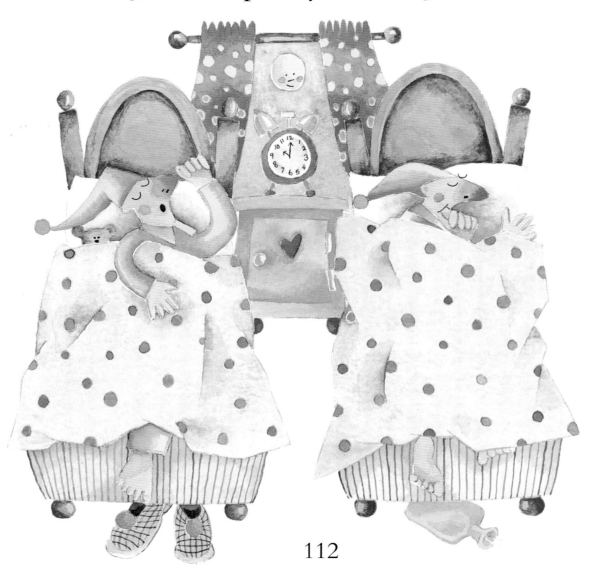

LITTLE TOMMY TITTLEMOUSE

Little Tommy Tittlemouse
Lived in a little house;
He caught fishes
In other men's ditches.

SEE-SAW, MARGERY DAW

See-saw, Margery Daw,
Jack shall have a new master;
He shall have but a penny a day,
Because he can't work any faster.

THREE YOUNG RATS

Three young rats with black felt hats,
Three young ducks with white straw flats,
Three young dogs with curling tails,
Three young cats with demi-veils,
Went out to walk with two young pigs
In satin vests and sorrel wigs;
But suddenly it chanced to rain,
And so they all went home again.

THE COLD OLD HOUSE

I know a house, and a cold old house,
A cold old house by the sea.
If I were a mouse in that cold old house
What a cold cold mouse I'd be!

THREE BLIND MICE

Three blind mice, see how they run!
Three blind mice, see how they run!
  They all ran after the farmer's wife,
Who cut off their tails with a carving-knife,
Did ever you hear such a thing in your life,
  As three blind mice.

BAT, BAT

Bat, Bat, come under my hat,
   And I'll give you a slice of bacon,
And when I bake I'll give you a cake,
   If I am not mistaken.

HICKORY, DICKORY, DOCK

Hickory, dickory, dock,
The mouse ran up the clock.
The clock struck one,
The mouse ran down,
Hickory, dickory, dock.

INTERY, MINTERY, CUTERY, CORN

Intery, mintery, cutery, corn,

Apple seed and apple thorn.

Wire, briar, limber, lock,

Three geese in a flock.

One flew east and one flew west;

One flew over the cuckoo's nest.

THE CUCKOO

Cuckoo, Cuckoo,
What do you do?
In April
I open my bill;
In May
I sing night and day;
In June
I change my tune;
In July
Away I fly;
In August
Away I must.

THERE WERE TWO BIRDS SAT ON A STONE

There were two birds sat on a stone,
  Fa, la, la, la, lal, de;
One flew away, then there was one,
  Fa, la, la, la, lal, de;
The other flew after, and then there
    was none,
  Fa, la, la, la, lal, de;
And so the poor stone was left all alone,
  Fa, la, la, la, lal, de!

TWO LITTLE DICKY BIRDS

Two little dicky birds sitting on a wall,
One named Peter, one named Paul.
Fly away, Peter!
Fly away, Paul!
Come back, Peter!
Come back, Paul!

THE WORLD

Great, wide, beautiful, wonderful World,
With the wonderful water round you curled,
And the wonderful grass upon your breast—
World, you are beautifully dressed.

The wonderful air is over me,
And the wonderful wind is shaking the tree,
It walks on the water, and whirls the mills,
And talks to itself on the tops of the hills.

You friendly Earth, how far do you go,
With the wheatfields that nod and the rivers that flow,
With cities and gardens, and cliffs, and isles,
And people upon you for thousands of miles?

Ah, you are so great, and I am so small,
I tremble to think of you, World, at all;
And yet, when I said my prayers today,
A whisper inside me seemed to say,
"You are more than the Earth, though you are such a dot:
You can love and think, and the Earth cannot."

WILLIAM BRIGHTY RANDS

122

ANSWER TO A CHILD'S QUESTION

Do you ask what the birds say? The sparrow, the dove,

The linnet and thrush say, "I love and I love!"

In the winter they're silent, the wind is so strong;

What it says I don't know, but it sings a loud song.

But green leaves, and blossoms, and sunny warm weather,

And singing and loving—all come back together.

But the lark is so brimful of gladness and love,

The green fields below him, the blue sky above,

That he sings, and he sings, and for ever sings he,

"I love my Love, and my Love loves me."

SAMUEL TAYLOR COLERIDGE

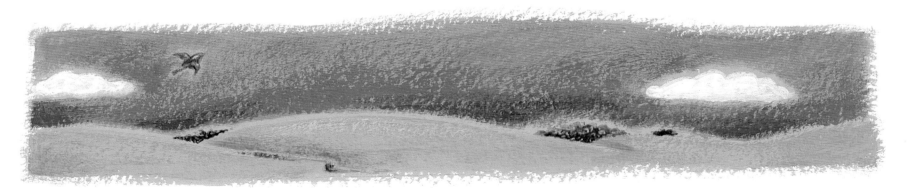

A WHITE HEN

A white hen sitting
  On white eggs three:
Next, three speckled chickens
  As plump as plump can be.

An owl and a hawk
  And a bat come to see;
But chicks beneath their mother's wing
  Squat safe as safe can be.

THE GRAND OLD DUKE OF YORK

The grand old Duke of York,
   He had ten thousand men;
He marched them up to the top of the hill,
   And he marched them down again!
And when they were up they were up,
   And when they were down they were down;
And when they were only halfway up,
   They were neither up nor down.

HUSH-A-BYE, BABY

Hush-a-bye, baby, on the tree top,
When the wind blows the cradle will rock;
When the bough breaks the cradle will fall,
Down will come baby, cradle and all.

ALL THE PRETTY LITTLE HORSES

Hush–a–bye, don't you cry,
Go to sleepy little baby.
When you wake
You shall have
All the pretty little horses.
Blacks and bays,
Dapples and greys,
Coach and six white horses.

Hush–a–bye, don't you cry,
Go to sleepy little baby.
When you wake
You shall have cake
And all the pretty little horses.

ROCK-A-BYE, BABY

Rock-a-bye, baby, thy cradle is green;

Father's a nobleman, Mother's a queen,

And Betty's a lady, and wears a gold ring,

And Johnny's a drummer, and drums for the King.

BYE, BABY BUNTING

Bye, baby bunting,
Father's gone a–hunting,
To fetch a little rabbit-skin
To wrap his baby bunting in.

COME TO BED, SAYS SLEEPY-HEAD

Come to bed,
Says Sleepy-head;
  "Tarry a while," says Slow;
"Put on the pot,"
Says Greedy-gut,
  "Let's sup before we go."

DIDDLE, DIDDLE, DUMPLING

Diddle, diddle, dumpling, my son John
Went to bed with his trousers on;
One shoe off, the other shoe on,
Diddle, diddle, dumpling, my son John.

131

LITTLE BOY BLUE

Little Boy Blue,
  Come blow your horn,
The sheep's in the meadow,
  The cow's in the corn.

Where is the boy
  Who looks after the sheep?
He's under a haycock
  Fast asleep.
Will you wake him?
  No, not I,
For if I do,
  He's sure to cry.

THERE WAS A LITTLE BOY

There was a little boy went into a barn,
And lay down on some hay;
An owl came out and flew about,
And the little boy ran away.

A SWARM OF BEES IN MAY

A swarm of bees in May
Is worth a load of hay;
A swarm of bees in June
Is worth a silver spoon;
A swarm of bees in July
Is not worth a fly.

WHAT DO THE STARS DO?

What do the stars do
  Up in the sky,
Higher than the wind can blow,
  Or the clouds can fly?

Each star in its own glory
  Circles, circles still;
As it was lit to shine and set,
  And do its Maker's will.

THE LILY HAS AN AIR

The lily has an air,
  And the snowdrop a grace,
And the sweetpea a way,
  And the heartsease a face—
Yet there's nothing like the rose
  When she blows.

PEASE-PUDDING HOT

Pease-pudding hot,
    Pease-pudding cold,
Pease-pudding in the pot,
    Nine days old.
Some like it hot,
    Some like it cold,
Some like it in the pot,
    Nine days old.

THE MAN IN THE MOON

The man in the moon,
  Came tumbling down,
And asked his way to Norwich.
  He went by the south,
  And burnt his mouth
With supping cold pease-porridge.

HIGGLETY, PIGGLETY, POP!

Higglety, piggelty, pop!
The dog has eaten the mop;
The pig's in a hurry,
The cat's in a flurry,
Higglety, piggelty, pop!

WE'RE ALL IN THE DUMPS

We're all in the dumps,
　For diamonds and trumps,
The kittens are gone to St. Paul's,
　The babies are bit,
　The moon's in a fit,
And the houses are built without walls.

RING-A-RING O' ROSES

Ring-a ring o' roses
　A pocket full of posies,
A-tishoo! A-tishoo!
　We all fall down.

THE MILLER OF DEE

There was a jolly miller
   Lived on the river Dee:
He worked and sung from morn till night,
   No lark so blithe as he;
And this the burden of his song
   For ever used to be—
I jump mejerrime jee!
   I care for nobody—no! not I,
Since nobody cares for me.

AS I WAS GOING ALONG

As I was going along, long, long,

A singing a comical song, song, song,

The lane that I went was so long, long, long,

And the song that I sung was as long, long, long,

And so I went singing along.

OVER THE HILLS AND FAR AWAY

When I was young and had no sense
I bought a fiddle for eighteenpence,
And the only tune that I could play
Was "Over the Hills and Far Away."

HEY, DIDDLE, DIDDLE

Hey, diddle, diddle, the cat and the fiddle,
The cow jumped over the moon;
The little dog laughed to see such sport,
And the dish ran away with the spoon!

GOOSEY, GOOSEY, GANDER

Goosey, goosey, gander,
  Whither shall I wander,
Upstairs, and downstairs,
  And in my lady's chamber.
There I met an old man,
  Who would not say his prayers,
I took him by his left leg
  And threw him down the stairs.

DAFFY-DOWN-DILLY

Daffy-
Down-
Dilly
has come
up to
town

In a
yellow
petticoat
and a
green
gown.

FROM WIBBLETON TO WOBBLETON

From Wibbleton to Wobbleton
  is fifteen miles,
From Wobbleton to Wibbleton
  is fifteen miles,
From Wibbleton to Wobbleton,
From Wobbleton to Wibbleton,
From Wibbleton to Wobbleton
  is fifteen miles.

146

SEE-SAW, SACRADOWN

See-saw, Sacradown,
Which is the way to London Town?
One foot up and one foot down,
That's the way to London Town.

HUMPTY DUMPTY

Humpty Dumpty sat on a wall,
Humpty Dumpty had a great fall;
All the king's horses and all the king's men
Couldn't put Humpty together again.

TWEEDLEDUM AND TWEEDLEDEE

Tweedledum and Tweedledee
   Agreed to have a battle,
For Tweedledum said Tweedledee
   Had spoiled his nice new rattle.
Just then flew down a monstrous crow,
   As big as a tar-barrel,
Which frightened both the heroes so,
   They quite forgot their quarrel.

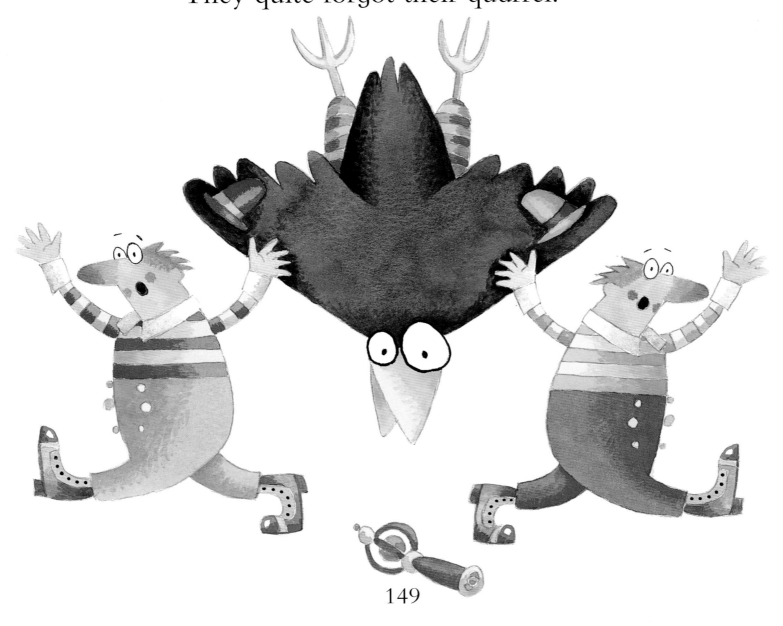

ROBIN THE BOBBIN

Robin the Bobbin, the big-bellied Ben,
He ate more meat than fourscore men;
He ate a cow, he ate a calf,
He ate a butcher and a half;
He ate a church, he ate a steeple,
He ate the priest and all the people!
A cow and a calf,
An ox and a half,
A church and a steeple,
And all the good people,
And yet he complained that his stomach wasn't full.

HECTOR PROTECTOR

Hector Protector was dressed all in green;
Hector Protector was sent to the Queen.
The Queen did not like him,
Nor more did the King;
So Hector Protector was sent back again.

FIVE LITTLE MONKEYS

Five little monkeys walked along the shore;

One went a-sailing,

Then there were four.

Four little monkeys climbed up a tree;

One of them tumbled down,

Then there were three.

Three little monkeys found a pot of glue;

One got stuck in it,

Then there were two.

Two little monkeys found a currant bun;

One ran away with it,

Then there was one.

One little monkey cried all afternoon,

So they put him in an airplane

And sent him to the moon.

THREE CHILDREN

Three children sliding on the ice
    Upon a summer's day,
As it fell out, they all fell in,
    The rest they ran away.

Now had these children been at home,
    Or sliding on dry ground,
Ten thousand pounds to one penny
    They had not all been drowned.

You parents all that children have,
    And you that have got none,
If you would have them safe abroad,
    Pray keep them safe at home.

A
RARE QUARRY

Two friends were out hunting otters and they walked beside a stream, looking at the banks for holes where the creatures might be hiding. Suddenly, one of them saw a flash of red. The creature moved quickly, darting along the bank and vanishing into a hole near a tree.

One friend turned to the other: "What was that? It was too large for a squirrel, too small for a fox. Could it be a rare, red-furred otter?"

The two men had never seen such an otter before, but could not think what other sort of creature it might be, so decided to try to catch it. They looked carefully at the burrow and saw that it had two entrances, one on either side of the tree. "We'll need a sack," said the first man, and he ran off to a nearby farm to borrow one.

When he returned, he held the sack over one end of the burrow, while his friend stood at the other end and made a noise to frighten the creature out. Sure enough, there was a mighty plop as the creature jumped into the sack. Holding the end closed, the two men made off for home, very pleased with their rare quarry.

The pair walked home across the fields, and had not gone very far when they were amazed to hear a tiny voice inside the sack calling "I hear my mother calling me. I hear my mother calling me." The men dropped the sack in astonishment and watched as a tiny figure climbed out. On his head was a red hat, and he wore pants and jacket and shoes that were also bright red. As he ran off towards the cover of some low bushes, again he looked like a streak of red, and the men saw how easy it had been to mistake him for an animal.

Looking at each other in alarm, the two hunters ran off towards home. They never hunted for otters again on that stretch of the river.

A CAT CAME FIDDLING OUT OF A BARN

A cat came fiddling out of a barn,
With a pair of bagpipes under her arm;
She could sing nothing but fiddle cum fee,
The mouse has married the humble-bee.
Pipe, cat—dance, mouse,
We'll have a wedding at our good house.

DING, DONG, BELL

Ding, dong, bell,
Pussy's in the well.
  Who put her in?
  Little Tommy Green.
Who pulled her out?
Little Tommy Trout.
  What a naughty boy was that,
  To try and drown poor pussy cat.
Who never did him any harm,
And killed the mice in his Father's barn.

FOLLOW MY BANGALOREY MAN

Follow my Bangalorey Man,
Follow my Bangalorey Man;
I'll do all that ever I can
To follow my Bangalorey Man.
We'll borrow a horse, and steal a gig,
And round the world we'll do a jig,
And I'll do all that ever I can
To follow my Bangalorey Man!

ANNA MARIA

Anna Maria she sat on the fire;

The fire was too hot, she sat on the pot;

The pot was too round, she sat on the ground;

The ground was too flat, she sat on the cat;

The cat ran away with Maria on her back.

159

HANDY SPANDY, JACK-A-DANDY

Handy Spandy, Jack-a-dandy
Loved plum cake and sugar candy;
He bought some at a grocer's shop,
And out he came, hop, hop, hop.

YANKEE DOODLE

Yankee Doodle went to town,
Riding on a pony;
He stuck a feather in his hat,
And called it macaroni.
 Yankee Doodle fa, so, la,
 Yankee Doodle dandy,
 Yankee Doodle fa, so, la,
 Buttermilk and brandy.

Yankee Doodle went to town
To buy a pair of pants
He swore he could not see the town
For so many houses.
 Yankee Doodle fa, so, la,
 Yankee Doodle dandy,
 Yankee Doodle fa, so, la,
 Buttermilk and brandy.

HARK! HARK!

Hark, hark,
The dogs do bark,
Beggars are coming to town:
Some in rags,
Some in tags,
And some in velvet gowns.

IF WISHES WERE HORSES

If wishes were horses,
    Beggars would ride;
If turnips were watches,
    I'd wear one by my side.

THE
LOST KINGDOM

In former times, the best land in Wales lay towards the West. The fertile plains and lush grasslands were fine country for farming, and all who worked these fields grew rich. But there was one problem with the country in the West. The ground lay so low that it was often flooded by the sea. So the kings of the West built a great wall, with strong sluice gates, to hold back the sea. For many years the people of the West enjoyed a life without floods, and they became the envy of all Wales.

One of the greatest of all the western kings was Gwyddno. Sixteen beautiful cities grew up in his kingdom while he reigned, and the lands of the West became more prosperous

than before. After the king, the most important person in the kingdom of the West was a man called Seithennin, whom Gwyddno appointed as the keeper of the sluices. Whenever a storm brewed, and the sea threatened to overwhelm the kingdom, Seithennin would close the great sluice gates, and the lands of the West would be safe.

Seithennin was a big, strong man, chosen because he could easily turn the handles to close the heavy oak sluice gates. But there was a problem. Seithennin was a drunkard. Sometimes, when he had had too much to drink, he would be late to close the gates, and there would be some slight flooding. But the kingdom would recover, and no great harm was done.

One day, King Gwyddno ordered a great banquet in his hall. All the lords and ladies of the kingdom were there, as well as other men of importance such as Seithennin. The banquet went on long into the night, and the sluice-keeper got more

and more drunk. There was singing and harping, and everyone was enjoying themselves to the full. But because of all the noise of the reveling, no one could hear that a great storm was brewing up outside. Even when people did start to notice, they assumed that Seithennin had closed the sluice gates and that they would be safe from flooding, as they had been for years now. But no one saw that the sluice-keeper, who had drunk more than anyone else at the banquet, was fast asleep.

Outside, the waters of the sea were pouring through the sluice gates. Soon the fields were flooded and the streets of the towns were awash. But still the banquet went on, until the flood waters poured through the doors of Gwyddno's hall. There had been floods in this part of Wales in earlier years, before the sea wall was built. Then people had lost their lives and good farm land had been spoiled.

But this time it was worse. The water poured in with such speed that it was unstoppable. Men, women, and children, lords and servants alike, were swept under the flood. Even those who knew the sea, including many fishermen who were excellent swimmers, lost their lives. Sheep and cattle went the same way. Soon the whole great kingdom of the West, every field and every town, was deep under the water. And all were drowned apart from one man, the poet Taliesin, who survived to tell the tale. They say that the sigh that Gwyddno let out as he was lost

under the waves was the saddest sound ever heard.

The sea now covers Gwyddno's former kingdom, in the place now called Cardigan Bay. Occasionally, at low tide, wooden posts and fragments of stone wall are revealed among the sand, and men say that these are the last remaining parts of one of Gwyddno's cities. Sailors and fishermen who cross the bay say that they can sometimes hear the bells of the sixteen cities, sounding beneath the waves, reminding them of the terrible power of the sea. Some even say that on a quiet, still day they can hear the echoing sound of Gwyddno's final sigh.

GIRLS AND BOYS COME OUT TO PLAY

Girls and boys, come out to play;

The moon doth shine as bright as day;

Leave your supper, and leave your sleep,

And come with your playfellows into the street.

Come with a whoop, come with a call,

Come with a good will or not at all.

Up the ladder and down the wall,

A halfpenny roll will serve us all.

You find milk, and I'll find flour,

And we'll have a pudding in half-an-hour.

GEORGIE, PORGIE

Georgie, Porgie, pudding and pie,
Kissed the girls and made them cry;
When the boys came out to play
Georgie Porgie ran away.

I SCREAM

I scream, you scream,
We all scream for ice cream!

CLUCK! CLUCK!

Cluck! cluck! the nursing hen
Summons her folk—
Ducklings all downy soft,
Yellow as yolk.

Cluck! cluck! the mother hen
Summons her chickens
To peck the dainty bits
Found in her pickings.

CHRISTINA ROSSETTI

A RACE

A daisy and a buttercup
Agreed to have a race,
A squirrel was to be the judge
A mile off from the place.

The squirrel waited patiently
Until the day was done.
Perhaps he is there waiting still,
You see, they couldn't run.

MARY LOUISA MOLESWORTH

THE MAN IN THE WILDERNESS

The man in the Wilderness asked me,
How many strawberries grew in the sea?
I answered him as I thought good,
As many red herrings as grew in the wood.

A PEANUT SAT ON THE RAILROAD TRACK

A peanut sat on the railroad track,
His heart was all a-flutter;
Along came a train—the 9:15—
Toot, toot, peanut butter!

THE QUEEN OF HEARTS

The Queen of Hearts, she made some tarts,
   All on a summer's day;
The Knave of Hearts, he stole the tarts,
   And took them clean away.

The King of Hearts called for the tarts,
   And beat the Knave full sore;
The Knave of Hearts brought back the tarts,
   And vowed he'd steal no more.

IF ALL THE WORLD WAS APPLE PIE

If all the world was apple pie,
And all the sea was ink,
And all the trees were bread and cheese,
What should we have for drink?

FOR WANT OF A NAIL

For want of a nail, the shoe was lost;
For want of the shoe, the horse was lost;
For want of the horse, the rider was lost;
For want of the rider, the battle was lost;
For want of the battle, the kingdom was lost;
And all from the want of a horseshoe nail.

175

THE

FENODEREE

On the Isle of Man lived a fairy who had been sent out of fairyland because he had had a passion for a mortal girl. The fairy folk found out about his love for the girl when he was absent from one of their gatherings. They found him dancing with his love in the merry Glen of Rushen. When the other fairies heard what he was doing, they cast a spell, forcing him to live for ever on the Isle of Man, and making him ugly and hairy. This is why people called him the Fenoderee, which means "hairy one" in the Manx language.

Although his appearance frightened people when they saw him, the Fenoderee was usually kind to humans, for he never forgot the girl he loved, and wanted to do what he could for her people. Sometimes he even helped people with their work, and used what was left of his fairy magic to carry out tasks which would have been exhausting for the strongest of men.

One thing the Fenoderee liked to do was to help the farmers in their fields. On one occasion he mowed a meadow for a farmer. But instead of being grateful, the farmer complained that the Fenoderee had not cut the grass short enough.

The Fenoderee was still sad at losing his mortal love, and angry that the farmer was so ungrateful, so next year at mowing time, he let the farmer do the job himself.

As the farmer walked along, swishing his scythe from side to side, the Fenoderee crept behind him, cutting up roots, and getting so close to the farmer that the man risked having his feet cut off.

When the farmer told this story, people knew that they should be grateful when the Fenoderee helped them with their work. So the custom arose of leaving the creature little gifts when he had been especially helpful.

On one occasion, a man was building himself a new house of stone. He found the stone he wanted on the cliffs by the beach, and paid some of the men of the parish to help him quarry it. There was one large block of fine marble which he especially wanted, but no matter how hard they tried, the block was too heavy to be moved, even if all the men of the parish tried to shift it.

Next day they were surprised to see that not only had the huge block of marble been carried to the building site, but all the other stone that the builder needed had been moved too.

At first, everyone wondered how the stone could have got there. But then someone said, "It must have been the Fenoderee who was working for us in the night." The builder

178

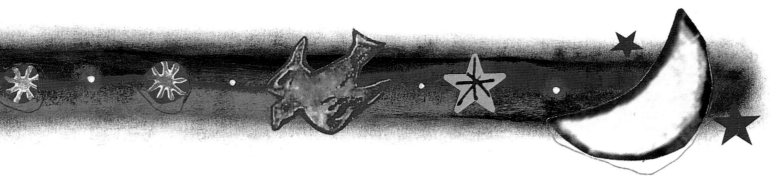

saw that this must be true, and thought that he should give the Fenoderee a handsome reward.

So he took some clothes of the right size for the creature, and left them in one of the places where he was sometimes seen.

That night, the Fenoderee appeared and found the clothes. Those who watched him were surprised at his sadness as he lifted each item up in turn and said these words:

Cap for the head, alas, poor head!

Coat for the back, alas, poor back!

Breeches for the breech, alas, poor breech!

If these all be thine, thine cannot be the merry glen of Rushen.

With these words, the Fenoderee walked away, and has never been seen since in that neighborhood.

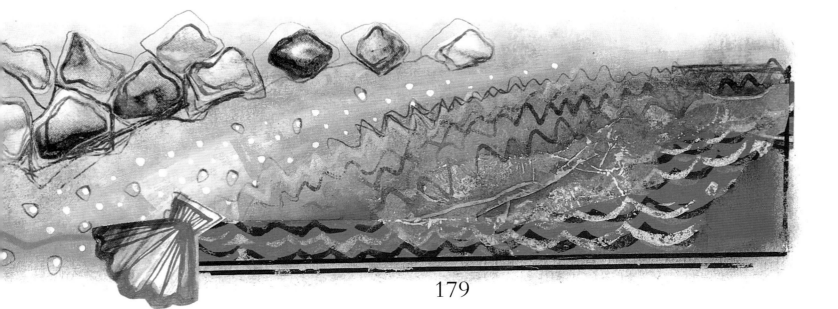

CALICO PIE

Calico Pie,

The little Birds fly

Down to the calico tree,

Their wings were blue,

And they sang "Tilly-loo!"

Till away they flew,—

And they never came back to me!

They never came back!

They never came back!

They never came back to me!

Calico Jam,

The little Fish swam,

Over the syllabub sea,

He took off his hat,

To the Sole and the Sprat,

And the Willeby-wat,—

But he never came back to me!

He never came back!

He never came back!

He never came back to me!

Calico Ban,

The little Mice ran,

To be ready in time for tea,

Flippity flup,

They drank it all up,

And danced in the cup,—

But they never came back to me!

They never came back!

They never came back!

They never came back to me!

Calico Drum,

The Grasshoppers come,

The Butterfly, Beetle, and Bee,

Over the ground,

Around and round,

With a hop and a bound,—

But they never came back!

They never came back!

They never came back!

They never came back to me!

EDWARD LEAR

DONKEY RIDING

Were you ever in Quebec,
Stowing timbers on a deck,
Where there's a king in his golden crown
   Riding on a donkey?

Hey ho, and away we go,
   Donkey riding, donkey riding,
Hey ho, and away we go,
   Riding on a donkey.

Were you ever in Cardiff Bay,
Where the folks all shout, Hooray!
Here comes John with his three months' pay,
   Riding on a donkey?

Hey ho, and away we go,
 Donkey riding, donkey riding,
Hey ho, and away we go,
 Riding on a donkey.

Were you ever off Cape Horn,
Where it's always fine and warm?
See the lion and the unicorn
 Riding on a donkey.

Hey ho, and away we go,
 Donkey riding, donkey riding,
Hey ho, and away we go,
 Riding on a donkey.

ANONYMOUS
ENGLISH SEA SHANTY

183

THE BUTTERFLY'S BALL

Come take up your hats, and away let us haste,
To the Butterfly's Ball, and the Grasshopper's Feast.
The trumpeter Gadfly has summoned the crew,
And the revels are now only waiting for you.

On the smooth-shaven grass by the side of a wood,
Beneath a broad oak which for ages has stood,
See the children of earth and the tenants of air,
For an evening's amusement together repair.

And there came the Beetle, so blind and so black,
Who carried the Emmet, his friend, on his back.
And there came the Gnat, and the Dragonfly too,
And all their relations, green, orange, and blue.

And there came the Moth, with her plumage of down,
And the Hornet, with jacket of yellow and brown;
Who with him the Wasp, his companion, did bring,
But they promised that evening, to lay by their sting.

Then the sly little Dormouse crept out of his hole,
And led to the feast his blind cousin the Mole.
And the Snail, with his horns peeping out of his shell,
Came, fatigued with the distance, the length of an ell.

A mushroom their table, and on it was laid
A water-dock leaf, which a tablecloth made.
The viands were various, to each of their taste,
And the Bee brought the honey to sweeten the feast.

With steps most majestic the Snail did advance,
And he promised the gazers a minuet to dance;
But they all laughed so loud that he drew in his head,
And went in his own little chamber to bed.

Then, as evening gave way to the shadows of night,
Their watchman, the Glowworm, came out with his light.
So home let us hasten, while yet we can see;
For no watchman is waiting for you and for me.

WILLIAM ROSCOE

A FRISKY LAMB

A frisky lamb
And a frisky child
Playing their pranks
  In a cowslip meadow:
The sky all blue
And the air all mild
And the fields all sun
  And the lanes half shadow.

ON THE GRASSY BANKS

On the grassy banks
Lambkins at their pranks;
Woolly sisters, woolly brothers,
  Jumping off their feet,
While their woolly mothers
  Watch by them and bleat.

THE WIND HAS SUCH
A RAINY SOUND

The wind has such a rainy sound
  Moaning through the town,
The sea has such a windy sound—
  Will the ships go down?

The apples in the orchard
  Tumble from their tree.
Oh will the ships go down, go down,
  In the windy sea?

SWIFT AND SURE
THE SWALLOW

Swift and sure the swallow,
  Slow and sure the snail:
Slow and sure may miss his way,
  Swift and sure may fail.

MAGPIES

One for sorrow, two for joy,
Three for a girl, four for a boy,
Five for silver, six for gold,
Seven for a secret never to be told.

LITTLE ROBIN REDBREAST

Little Robin Redbreast
   Sat upon a rail:
Niddle-noddle went his head!
   Wiggle-waggle went his tail.

THE NORTH WIND DOTH BLOW

The north wind doth blow,
And we shall have snow,
And what will poor Robin do then?
                    Poor thing!

He'll sit in a barn,
And to keep himself warm,
Will hide his head under his wing.
                    Poor thing!

A CHRISTMAS CAROL

In the bleak midwinter
  Frosty wind made moan,
Earth stood hard as iron,
  Water like a stone;
Snow had fallen, snow on snow,
  Snow on snow,
In the bleak midwinter
  Long ago.

Our God, heaven cannot hold Him,
  Nor earth sustain;
Heaven and earth shall flee away
  When He comes to reign:
In the bleak midwinter
  A stable-place sufficed
The Lord God Almighty,
  Jesus Christ.

What can I give him,
   Poor as I am?
If I were a shepherd
   I would bring a lamb;
If I were a wise man
   I would do my part—
Yet what I can, I give Him,
   Give my heart.

CHRISTINA ROSSETTI

IF THE MOON CAME
FROM HEAVEN

If the moon came from heaven,
  Talking all the way,
What could she have to tell us,
  And what could she say?

"I've seen a hundred pretty things,
  And seen a hundred gay;
But only think: I peep by night
  And do not peep by day!"

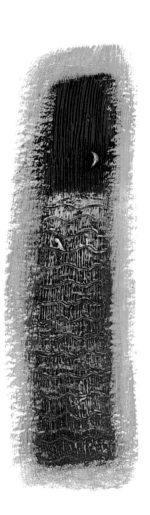

IS THE MOON TIRED?

Is the moon tired? she looks so pale
  Within her misty veil:
She scales the sky from east to west,
  And takes no rest.